A long time ago in a little farmhouse, there lived two sisters. Their names were Rose and Betsy. Rose was the oldest, and she was mean. The younger one was called Betsy, and she was the good sister.

The two sisters were not treated the same. Betsy had to do all of the chores, while Rose was allowed to sit on the porch and daydream all the time. It was not right.

While Betsy was out in the forest tending to the chickens one morning, she met an old maid who was very thirsty. Being a friendly girl, Betsy fetched the maid a drink from the well on her family's farm.

But helping the thirsty old maid made Betsy late, and she got told off when she got home. Her family shouted at her. They made her so frightened that she ran away. She went back out into the forest, where she saw the old maid again.

The old maid took Betsy to an old shack deep in the woods. Before she opened the door, she told Betsy not to make fun of anything she saw inside. To Betsy's surprise, inside the shack was a cow with two heads and corkscrew horns, rabbits in shirts, and some very odd-looking chickens with three legs!

Betsy helped the old maid collect firewood and make a stew. Then they ate and drank, and had a party with all of the odd animals. Betsy stayed the night in the shack. She slept well, and had sweet dreams.

In the morning, Betsy milked the two-headed cow, and drank its creamy milk. Then she went to the chicken coop.

The old maid told Betsy, “Take only the eggs that say ‘take me’ and leave the eggs that say ‘do not take me.’”

All of the eggs that said "take me" were small and dull, and all of the eggs that said "do not take me" were big and bright, but Betsy did as she was told and took the dull eggs. Then as she was walking home, all of the dull little eggs cracked open and wonderful gifts popped out!

Betsy rushed home with her gifts. There were gold coins, fine dresses, and silver bangles. When her family saw the fine gifts, they helped Betsy inside. For the first time in her life, Betsy's family were not cross with her.

But that night while Betsy was asleep, Rose and the rest of her family came up with a wicked plan to go to the old maid's shack and steal all of the talking eggs.

The next morning, Rose went to the shack in the forest. She told the old maid, "I am Betsy's sister," and the old maid welcomed her in.

Inside the shack, Rose pointed and chuckled at the two-headed cow, the rabbits in shirts, and the three-legged chickens. The old maid shook her head sadly.

Then the old maid took Rose to the chicken coop. She told Rose the same thing she had told Betsy, "Take only the eggs that say 'take me.'"

But Rose was a selfish girl. She took all of the big, bright eggs that said "do not take me."

As Rose ran off into the woods with her stolen eggs, the eggs cracked and all manner of terrifying things popped out. There were angry bees, horrible snakes, and poisonous toads. All of the angry animals chased, bit, and stung Rose.

When Rose reached her home, her family tried to fight off the angry animals with brooms and wooden spoons, but that just made the animals attack them as well! The angry animals chased the family out of the farm and into the woods, attacking them all the way. Only Betsy was left unharmed and at home.

When Rose and her family got back to the farmhouse, it was the middle of the night. They were tired and sore, with bites and stings all over.

"Betsy, Betsy! Come and help us," they shouted.

But Betsy was nowhere to be seen.

Betsy had left her home and gone to the next big town, where she spent all of her gold coins on a big house. She took in stray animals, made many friends, and she lived out her days happily – unlike her greedy, mean family!